ISBN-13: 978-1519353313

ISBN-10: 1519353316

D1444607

Thank you Pastor Brian, Judy
and Mom for teaching me
about God.

God knows what
we do not see,

When we see a mess of threads, yarn, and some squares.

God sees life's quilt made
from all of its layers.

When we see a mountain too hard to climb,

God helps us climb it
but in His own time.

When we see a tree
that has nothing to bare,

God sees His apples
growing up in the air.

When we see seeds scattered
all over the ground,

When we see a rock wall
blocking our way,

God sees a barrier to guard us someday.

God always gives us
choices to make,

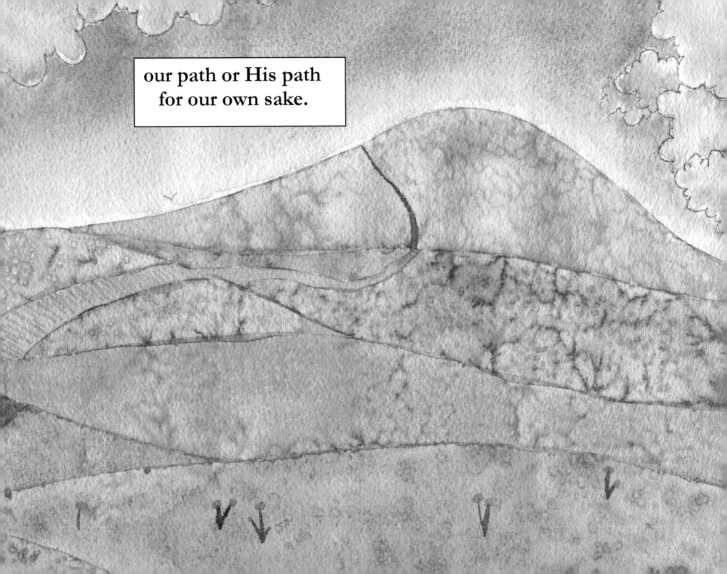

our path or His path
for our own sake.

When we see a door
closed very tight,

God sees a window
right in our sight.

When we see caterpillars
crawling on leaves.

God sees His butterflies gliding in the breeze.

When we think our countless ideas are great,

God knows His ideas are
best when we wait.

When we see rose stems
all covered in thorns;

God sees His flowers
in all of their forms.

When we see an obstacle
impossible to cross;

When we see our world
is about to unwind,.

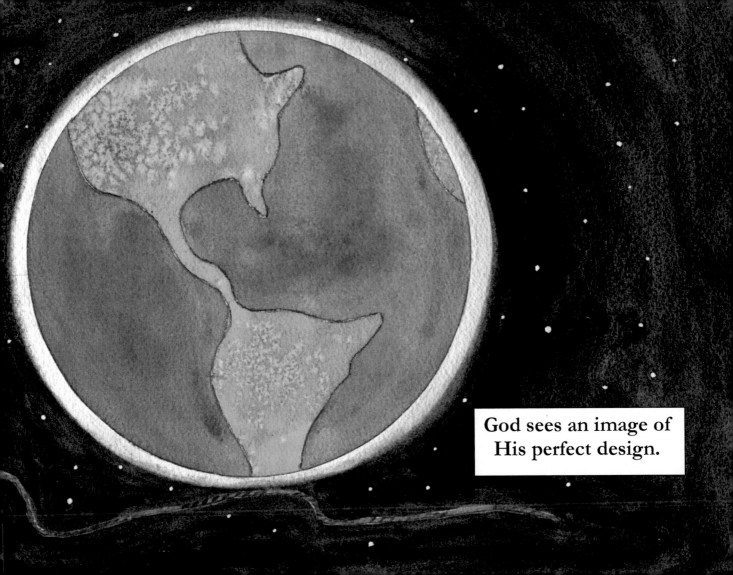

God sees an image of
His perfect design.

When we see grey clouds and lightning causing a storm;

God shows us His rainbow
in its most beautiful form.

Trust in the Lord with
all your heart
and lean not on your
own understanding;
in all your ways
acknowledge Him,
and He will make your
paths straight.

Proverbs 3:5&6

Made in the USA
Middletown, DE
09 April 2017

ISBN 9781519353313

90000

9 781519 353313